The original radio story of **THE CINNAMON BEAR** was inspired by the stuffed bear of Glan Heisch's own boyhood. When his first daughter, Catherine, came along, he started writing light verse for her, and naturally, one story was about his old friend, Paddy O'Cinnamon. **THE CINNAMON BEAR** was a labor of love, as listeners have known down through the years.

This book was given to

_____

By _____

Date _____

Text and Illustrations © 1991
All rights reserved. Published by Zack Press
an Imprint of Stiles-Bishop Productions Inc.,
P.O. Box 93531, Los Angeles, Ca. 90093-0531
Printed in Los Angeles.

Library of Congress Cataloging-in-Publication Data applied for.
ISBN 1-880623-01-3

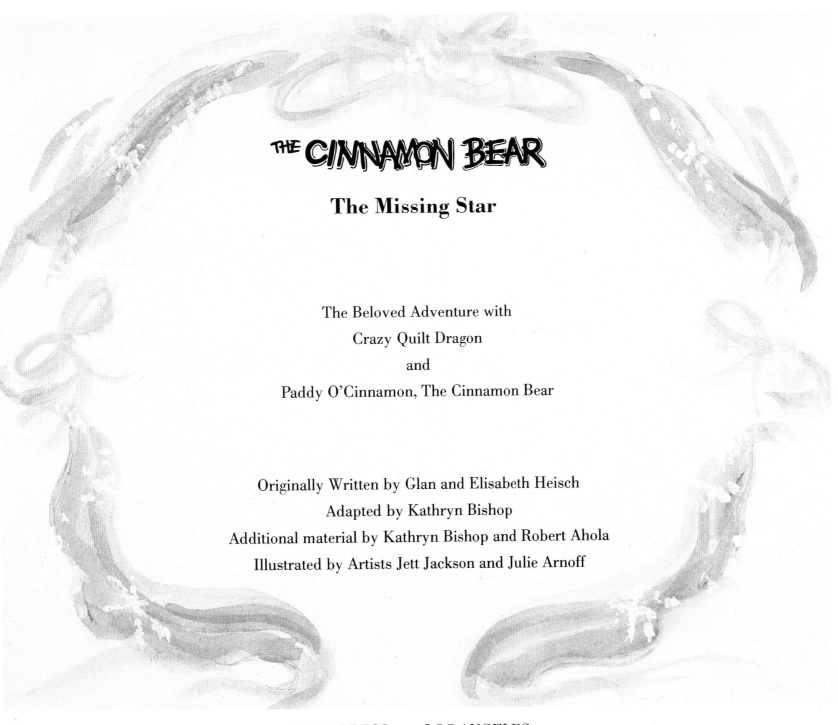

THE CINNAMON BEAR

The Missing Star

The Beloved Adventure with
Crazy Quilt Dragon
and
Paddy O'Cinnamon, The Cinnamon Bear

Originally Written by Glan and Elisabeth Heisch
Adapted by Kathryn Bishop
Additional material by Kathryn Bishop and Robert Ahola
Illustrated by Artists Jett Jackson and Julie Arnoff

ZACK PRESS   LOS ANGELES

This first book about Paddy 'O'Cinnamon has been a special joy for us to bring to print. We wish to thank Glan Heisch, Elisabeth Heisch, Randolph Stiles, Eileen Wasserman, Susan Noel Benfatto, Kathryn Leigh Scott and my parents, Muriel and Quentin Leisher, for their encouragement, support, editorial suggestions and advice. It was my mother who tuned our radio to this special story when I was a child. And a special **thank you** to my son, Zachary, who inspired me this year by his genuine enjoyment of the story of Paddy O'Cinnamon.

K.B.

Judy and Jimmy Barton were helping their mom decorate their Christmas tree. Judy eagerly searched the big ornament box. "Mom, the silver star for the top of our tree is missing!" Judy shouted.

"It's probably still up in the attic," Mom said.

Quickly, Judy and Jimmy ran up the stairs. "Look in Grandpa's trunk," called Mom.

Inside the old trunk, they found a toy plane, an old quilt of many colors and a tiny teddy bear... but no star. Jimmy was very upset. "Christmas just won't be Christmas without our star at the top of tree," he said sadly.

Suddenly a tiny voice called out, "I know where your star is."

Judy and Jimmy looked at each other. Who had spoken?

"It's me, Paddy O'Cinnamon," said the little old teddy bear. He began to sing, "I'm the Cinnamon Bear with the shoe-button eyes and I'm looking for someone to take by surprise."

Well, he sure surprised Judy and Jimmy. "Can you help us find our star, Paddy?" asked Jimmy. "This year it's my turn to put it on top of the tree."

"No it's not," shouted Judy. "It's my turn!"

"Now stop that," said Paddy firmly. "If you want something badly enough, you start by believing in yourself. Then try your hardest and never give up! Like magic, you can gain anything you desire," he finished with a wise smile.

"Even our star?" asked Judy.

"I will help you," he said shyly and winked. "I think Crazy Quilt has taken your star to Maybeland."

"Who's Crazy Quilt?" asked Jimmy.

"Crazy Quilt is a sticky-fingered dragon who always steals shiny things. He really liked your star."

"Where's Maybeland?" interrupted Jimmy.

"It's through that knothole," Paddy replied.

Judy almost dropped Paddy. "We're too big!" she gasped.

"That's only because you see yourself that way," explained Paddy. Then he chanted in rhyme, "Just ... blink your eyes, tap your toes, pull on my green bow, and we'll all degrow!"

Suddenly, Judy, Jimmy and Paddy all shrunk to the size just right for the plane. "How did you do that?" asked Judy, full of amazement.

"I believed in myself," replied Paddy. "If you see yourself small, you will be small. If you see yourself tall, you will be tall. By using my mind and my magic bow there isn't anything I can't do."

Judy and Jimmy could hardly believe their eyes.

"Come on," said Paddy smiling. "Stop staring and hop in."

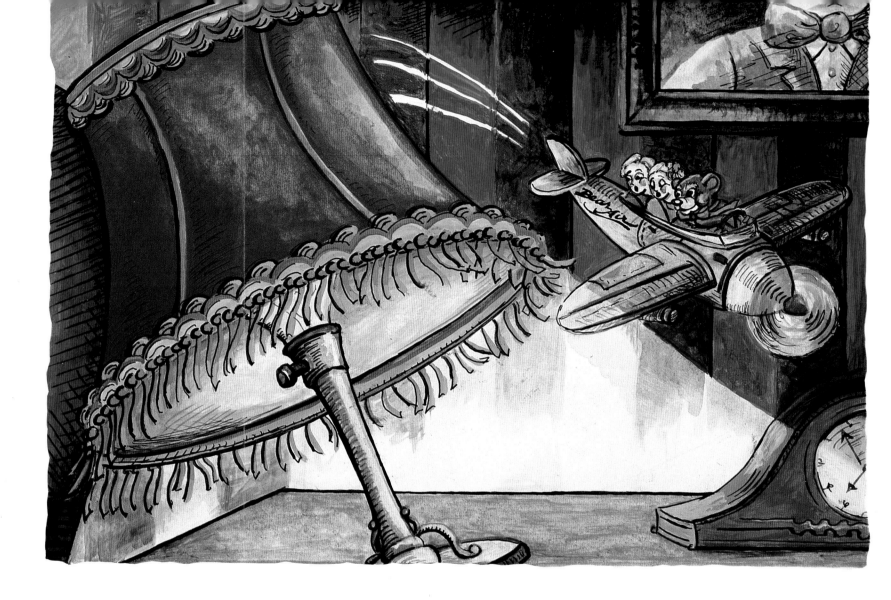

The plane hadn't been used in a long time, but finally it sputtered and roared to life. Soon they were flying swiftly through the attic. Paddy was so happy and excited to be helping someone that he got a bit careless.

"Watch out!" Judy cried.

The plane almost hit the old lamp shade before Paddy regained control.

"Whew, that was a close one," whispered Jimmy.

The plane circled around the attic one more time and then dove into the knothole — past the nails and the boards and into the darkness.

"First we fly over the Sea of Doubt," explained Paddy. "We must be very careful there. If we don't really believe in ourselves then we'll never make it. Then, on these Wings of Expectation, more commonly known as 'Bear Air', we'll go to the Land of Imagination. Right in the middle is Maybeland."

The plane set down on Lollipop Mountain, the highest point in Maybeland, and rolled to a stop. Nearby, Crazy Quilt Dragon was playing his silver piano.

"I just get crazy, c-c-c-c-crazy, c-c-c-c-crazy, I'm a super star," sang the Dragon in all of his multi-colored, quilted splendor. His tasseled tail beat out the rhythm of his song.

Paddy, Judy and Jimmy crept up behind Crazy Quilt as he held the star to his face like a mirror. They jumped in front of Crazy Quilt and shouted, "Give us our star!"

Crazy Quilt quickly tucked the star into one of his many patch pockets. "I don't have your old star," replied Crazy Quilt indignantly.

Paddy angrily pushed his chest out and stretched up to his full height. "Shame on you for lying, Crazy Quilt!" he said sternly.

    With that, Crazy Quilt jumped up and ran for the top of the mountain. He zigged and zagged through the lollipops to avoid Paddy, Judy and Jimmy, who were almost upon him.

    As Crazy Quilt made a quick turn, the star flew out of his pocket. He tried to grab for it but the star slipped out of his hands. Suddenly, Crazy Quilt and the star fell head over heels off the side of the mountain. They tumbled through the air, down towards the Root Beer Ocean.

HONK!

HONK!

BEEP!

BEEP!

CRASH!!

Paddy, Judy and Jimmy raced down the mountain to the beach. But all they could find were some crashed toy cars and a Roly Poly Policeman. "Please Mr. Policeman," inquired Judy politely, "have you seen our missing star?"

"My yes," replied the Roly Poly Policeman. "I caught a star about two hours ago... or was it two days ago... or was it two minutes ago. Oh my, oh my, sometimes I feel so confused. Oh my, oh yes, I remember, I gave it to a wonderful fellow who said it was his."

"Could he have been a dragon?" asked Paddy.

"Oh yes, oh yes, charming fellow he was too," said Roly Poly, as he pointed out the way Crazy Quilt went.

So Paddy, Judy and Jimmy set off. They walked and walked for hours down the beach. "Which way should we go now?" asked Judy, feeling a bit uncertain when she saw a cave.

"Follow your nose," said Paddy confidently.

"Oh Paddy," whined Jimmy, "That's just something people say when they're not sure."

"No it's not," said Paddy as he walked up to the cave. My nose knows which way to go." He bent down at the cave's opening and picked up a strand of red yarn. "A piece of Crazy Quilt's tail. This way, kids," shouted Paddy as he disappeared into the cave.

The three adventurers moved slowly into the cave. "It's dark and smelly in here," complained Jimmy. His voice echoed strangely.

Judy screamed.

She was falling.
Jimmy grabbed for Paddy.
They were falling too.

They tumbled out of the cave and landed on a bed of soft green moss. Right before them stood a wavy-roofed, crooked cottage. As Paddy started to knock on the door, it opened by itself. "It's magic," Jimmy whispered.

Paddy, Judy and Jimmy tiptoed timidly into the empty room. It had absolutely no furniture. On the far wall was a big gold picture frame surrounding a painting of the most beautiful forest they'd ever seen.

Judy stepped closer to the forest picture and said, "It looks so real, like I could just step into it." In the picture, there was Crazy Quilt, collapsed at the base of a big tree. Without thinking, she stepped right into the painting.

Paddy and Jimmy looked at each other. They each took a deep breath and jumped into the painting too.

"Oh, my head," moaned Crazy Quilt. "She hypnotized me and took the star!"

"She who?" demanded Paddy.

"Oh, no," cried Jimmy, as he grabbed Judy's arm.

"Oh, yes," declared the Wintergreen Witch, looming behind them. "I've got your precious star and now it is mine. I'll never give it back! It will shine in my magic forest forever."

Judy and Jimmy rushed toward the hideous woman.

"Back off!" screamed the Witch. "Or I'll turn you into frozen statues right now!" She shrieked and leapt out of the picture of the Magic Forest.

A huge set of jail bars suddenly crashed down. Paddy, Jimmy, Judy and Crazy Quilt were prisoners! The Wintergreen Witch tossed the Silver Star to Judy. "Here my sweet, spend your last night with your precious star," and she turned and disappeared through a wall.

It was late that night. Judy and Jimmy nervously looked at Paddy. "Now?" Judy asked in a whisper. Paddy nodded and everyone touched his magic green bow. "Blink your eyes, tap your toes, pull on my bow!" And ... suddenly they were all even smaller. Tiny enough to slip through the bars. Carefully, they tiptoed.

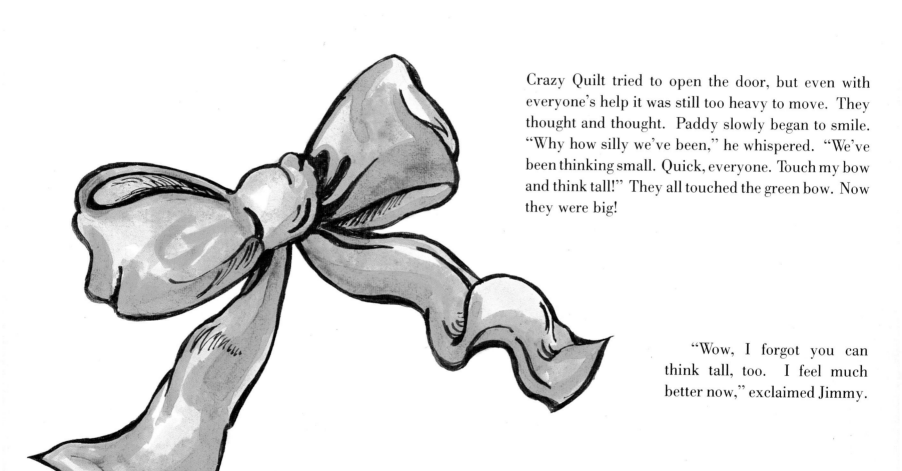

Crazy Quilt tried to open the door, but even with everyone's help it was still too heavy to move. They thought and thought. Paddy slowly began to smile. "Why how silly we've been," he whispered. "We've been thinking small. Quick, everyone. Touch my bow and think tall!" They all touched the green bow. Now they were big!

"Wow, I forgot you can think tall, too. I feel much better now," exclaimed Jimmy.

They carefully tiptoed out of the house, but as Crazy Quilt tried to close the door quietly, it slammed shut with a loud bang.

The Wintergreen Witch appeared at her door, screaming as they ran into the woods. She hopped on her laser broom and chased Crazy Quilt through the trees.

Suddenly she lowered her broom and fired a bolt of lightning. It shot through the forest and sliced a tree in half. The falling tree missed Crazy Quilt's tail by inches! Flying recklessly as she cackled, the Wintergreen Witch crashed into the tree.

Crazy Quilt didn't even look behind him. All he and the others wanted to do was to get away. They ran as fast as their legs would go.

"Let's stop," said Jimmy, "I'm exhausted." They had been running for a long time and the Witch was not behind them anymore.

Crazy Quilt, of course, collapsed immediately and picked a nice big rock on which to rest his weary body. Crack!!! It was an awful sound from his back pocket. Crazy slowly removed four pieces of the star.

"It's broken," cried Judy. "Oh, Jimmy, I give up! Let's just go home."

"Oh no, you mustn't give up now. We've come so far together. You must believe that we will succeed," said Paddy. "We'll go to Melissa, the Queen of Maybeland. She'll know how to fix the star."

Crazy Quilt stood up and shouted, "Hop on and we'll be off!" Paddy, Jimmy, and Judy climbed up Crazy Quilt's ridges, and off they went to find Queen Melissa.

After what seemed like forever, the castle of Melissa, Queen of Maybeland, came into view. It was so beautiful, it seemed to glow. At the drawbridge they met a strange looking, oddly dressed little man. "Welcome to Maybeland," he said, as he bowed and swept his big fancy hat to the ground. "I'm the Grand Wunky, Queen Melissa's Prime Minister, occasional escort, and chief fixer-upper."

"We're in quite a rush," interrupted Crazy Quilt.

"Now, now, you all look very shabby. You can't be seeing Melissa dressed like that. I have some garments you can buy," continued the Grand Wunky.

Paddy spoke up. "The kids have to get home soon. I'm sure Melissa will understand if we only brush off our clothes."

"Well, I'm not sure..." he complained as they smoothed their clothes. When the Grand Wunky was finally satisfied, he led them up the big white curving staircase.

At the top of the staircase was a huge white room with many white columns and the beautiful Queen Melissa seated on her golden throne.

They introduced themselves and told her of their adventure and the broken star. Queen Melissa took the four pieces and looked them over carefully. "The Witch's evil powers have made the star very brittle. Your only hope is to go to the Well of One Wish."

"Oh thank you, Queen Melissa," said Crazy Quilt.

"Wintergreen is very greedy and mean, so you must be very careful," explained Queen Melissa, "But I'll tell you a secret. If Wintergreen tries to hurt you in any way, simply show her the pieces of the star."

"Give them to her?" asked Judy.

"No, just show them to her. Now take this Wishing Well coin and off you go," said Queen Melissa, as she rose and walked them to the door.

As they left the castle, the Grand Wunky tried to sell them a map to the Well of One Wish. Paddy declined graciously because he had seen the clearly posted road signs. Crazy Quilt laughed at the Grand Wunky's feeble efforts to make his fortune.

They began to jog and sing together. "He's the Cinnamon Bear with the shoe-button eyes and he's looking for someone to help and delight."

They were all having so much fun they didn't even notice the strange green bush that slyly reached out and slipped Paddy's green bow from around his neck. Paddy was too busy pointing out the Well of One Wish which was right up ahead.

At the well, Crazy Quilt took the four pieces out of his pocket as he read the posted sign. "It says, 'Be your party one or eight, just one wish is all you rate!' That's too bad," he chuckled.

"We could use another wish to get rid of that awful witch," laughed Judy.

"Oh, yeah?" boomed a loud cackle.

"Wintergreen!" Crazy Quilt yelled and shook with fright. Paddy jumped up on the ledge of the well to challenge the Wintergreen Witch eye to eye.

Wintergreen laughed and poked one long bony finger into Paddy's stomach, forcing him backwards on the well's edge. Paddy tried to keep his balance, but he slipped on the wet bricks and fell into the well.

The sides of the well were slippery and gooey. The bottom was quicksand. "Help! I'm sinking!" shrieked Paddy.

"Use your green bow, you fool," yelled Crazy Quilt as he and Judy and Jimmy ran to the edge.

Paddy grabbed at his neck, desperately searching for his bow.

Wintergreen laughed. "He can't. I have it."

"We'll just use our wish," said Judy.

"No," said Crazy Quilt, "You have to save it for the star."

"Use your wish however you want, my silly children. Because I'm going to take the star too," cackled the Wintergreen Witch.

Judy looked at Jimmy. He nodded. She closed her eyes. She wished that Paddy would be safe and sound and on the ground right next to her. Then she threw Melissa's coin into the well.

When she opened her eyes, Paddy was standing right next to her! His green bow was around his neck, just as good as ever!

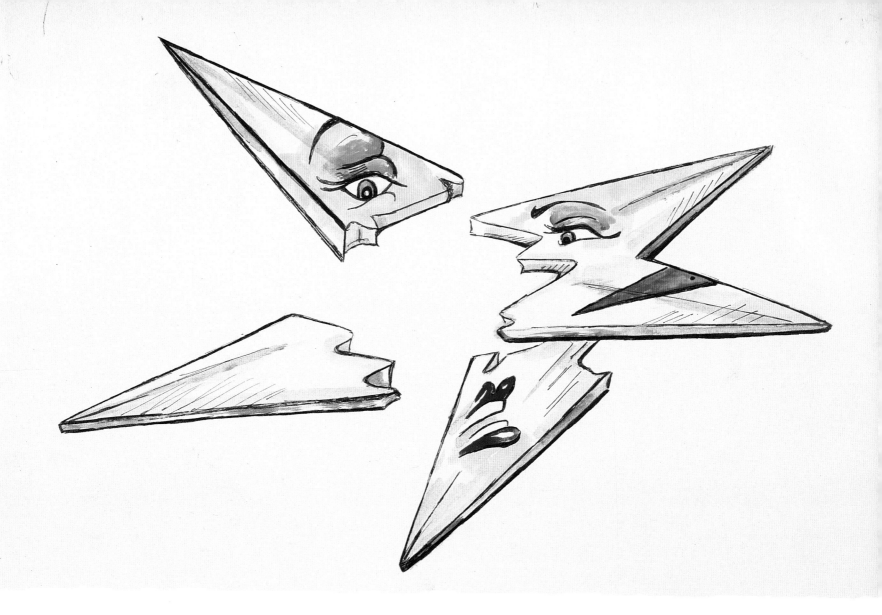

"So you used your only wish. Good, now I'll take that star," demanded the Wintergreen Witch.

"Remember what our pretty friend said," whispered Paddy. Crazy Quilt quickly gave each of his three friends a piece of the star.

"Stop stalling. Give me the star," screamed the Witch.

So Judy, Jimmy, Paddy and Crazy held their pieces up to Wintergreen's ugly face. For a moment nothing happened. Then the Witch screamed. It was the most horrible cry Judy had ever heard. Suddenly, the Wintergreen Witch disappeared in a puff of smoke.

Judy looked closely at her piece of the star. "Mirrors!" exclaimed Judy. "She saw her ugly face in the mirrors!"

"She's gone. Hooray!" yelled Jimmy.

'Yes, but the star is still broken," said Crazy Quilt. "We'll have to give up."

"No need to do that," exclaimed the Grand Wunky. He crawled out from under a hedge. "Queen Melissa sent me to keep an eye on you. I can see you do need my help."

He led them to Paddy's plane, 'Bear Air', on Lollipop Mountain.

"No maps to sell?" asked Crazy Quilt.

"Queen Melissa is curtailing my activities a bit, but I do think I should add a line of mirrors to my merchandise," replied the Grand Wunky.

Crazy Quilt laughed. Grand Wunky continued, "Buckle your seat belts, and someone who can fix your star will meet you."

"Meet us where?" asked Paddy, as he started the plane. He never got an answer, because suddenly the plane took off, flying faster and faster through the clouds. Then, just as suddenly, it landed in snow!

They all climbed out and followed the snow-covered walk to the front door of a big icicle-covered house. A skinny, wizened-faced man with ice-blue eyes and icicles for hair answered Paddy's knock. "Hi, I've been expecting you. I'm Jack Frost."

Jimmy was speechless as they all followed Jack Frost into the strange living room. The walls were made of ice. The lamps hung from icicles. You could ice skate on the floor.

"Could you possibly help us fix our star, Mr. Frost?" asked Judy. "We'd be very grateful and we've come so far – please help us!"

"Well, let me have a look," said Jack Frost thoughtfully. He took the star pieces and went to work immediately. Powdery sparkling dust floated through the air as the star pieces were polished by the strange, whirling machines. Then Jack Frost rubbed his icy finger on every edge. He held the pieces together for just a second, and the star was glued back together! He showed them the beautiful restored star and set it on an open window sill to dry.

Everyone was amazed. "How can we ever thank you?" asked Judy.

"No thanks needed. I'm just proud to be of help," replied Jack. "Come, I'll show you some of my most fantastic ice creations." Turning to Paddy, he said, "I heard that you like cinnamon rolls, Paddy, so we made some especially for you."

"Your reward, Paddy," Judy giggled.

"By the way," asked Jack Frost, "Where's Crazy Quilt?"

They all turned at the same time and looked at the open window.

The star was gone. Through the open window, they could see Crazy Quilt Dragon running across the snow.

"Oh no, not again," moaned Jimmy. Paddy and Judy were yelling at Crazy Quilt as they chased after him towards the North Pole.

Crazy Quilt started climbing the North Pole itself. Judy, Jimmy and Paddy climbed up right behind him. They all were so heavy that the pole started to sway. Slowly, back and forth, back and forth, wider and wider it swung. Crazy Quilt lost his grip and fell, covering them with his body.

The big old quilt was a huge lump on the floor. As she lifted the edge, Mom said, "Wake up, you sleepyheads. Let's get this tree decorated. I see you found the star. That's terrific."

Judy and Jimmy surfaced from under the quilt. Judy had the star. Jimmy clutched Paddy tightly.

"Where did you find him?" Mom asked. She stroked the top of Paddy's head. "I haven't seen him since I was about your age."

Mom started to sing softly, "He's the Cinnamon Bear, with the shoe-button eyes, and he's looking for someone to take by surprise."

Judy dragged Jimmy down the stairs. She didn't want to tell her mother about their adventure — not yet.

In the living room, Dad stood near the top of the ladder. The tree was almost finished. "You two are very quiet tonight."

"I think they had an exciting dream this afternoon," said Mom.

Judy and Jimmy looked at each other. It was an adventure with Paddy O'Cinnamon, not a dream. They just knew it was real!

"Well," Dad asked, "who gets to put the star on top of the tree this year?"

"Jimmy's turn," announced Judy, being the generous sister for the first time.

Jimmy gave Judy his biggest, most beautiful smile, and then ran to the ladder. Dad and Mom were amazed. This was the first year that Judy and Jimmy hadn't fought over the star. Judy picked up Paddy from the couch. She gave him a big hug and gently placed him on a big tree branch.

"Thanks, Paddy," she whispered, "Have a Merry Christmas."